THIS CANDLEWICK BOOK BELONGS TO:

_____

_____

_____

_____

For the Rainy Lake writers,

who know what writers want

P. R.

For Pat,

in memory of Paddy

J. B.

First U.S. paperback edition 2001

The Library of Congress has cataloged the hardcover edition as follows:

Root, Phyllis.
What Baby wants / Phyllis Root ; illustrated by Jill Barton. — 1st U.S. ed.
p.   cm.
Summary: Various family members try to stop Baby from crying, but only his brother figures out what he wants.
ISBN 0-7636-0207-8 (hardcover)
[1. Babies — Fiction.] I. Barton, Jill, ill. II. Title.
PZ7.R6784Wh   1998
[E] — dc21   97-40424
ISBN 0-7636-1263-4 (paperback)

2 4 6 8 10 9 7 5 3 1

Printed in Hong Kong

This book was typeset in Cochin.
The illustrations were done in watercolor.

Candlewick Press
2067 Massachusetts Avenue
Cambridge, Massachusetts 02140

What Baby Wants

Phyllis Root

illustrated by Jill Barton

CANDLEWICK PRESS
CAMBRIDGE, MASSACHUSETTS

Mama was tired,
but Baby wouldn't sleep.

"Don't worry," said
Grandma and Grandpa
and Aunt and Uncle
and Big Sister and
Little Brother.
"We'll take care of
Baby for you."

So Mama fed Baby,
tucked him in his cradle,
and went to bed.

WAAAAAH! said Baby.

"I know what Baby wants!"
said Grandma.
"Baby wants something
pretty to look at."

So Grandma went out to the meadow

and brought Baby an armload of flowers.
Was that what Baby wanted?

Pikala, pokala, the flowers prickled Baby's nose.

WAAAAAH! said Baby.

"I know what Baby wants!"
said Grandpa.
"Baby wants something
soft to cuddle."

So Grandpa went out to the barnyard

and brought Baby a soft feathery goose.
Was that what Baby wanted?

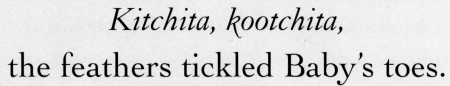

Kitchita, kootchita,
the feathers tickled Baby's toes.

WAAAAAH! said Baby.

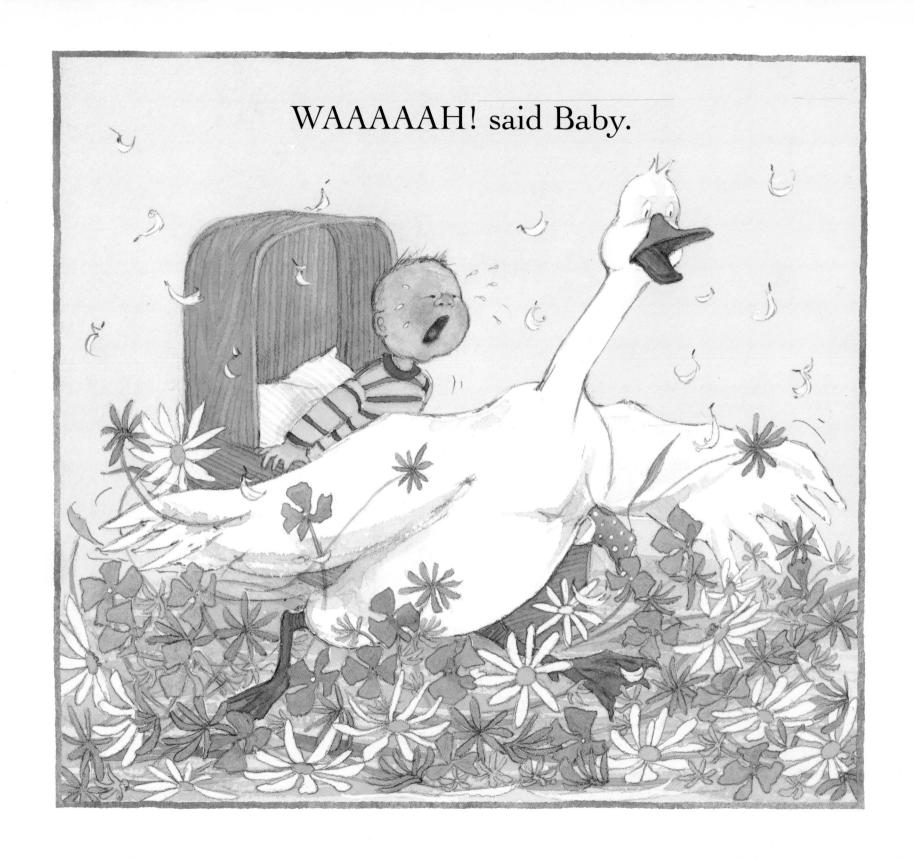

"I know what Baby wants!" said Aunt.
"Baby wants a great big kiss."

So Aunt went out to the field

and brought Baby a cow to kiss him
with her long tongue.
Was that what Baby wanted?

Slurpilla, sloppilla,
the cow slobbered
on Baby's chin.

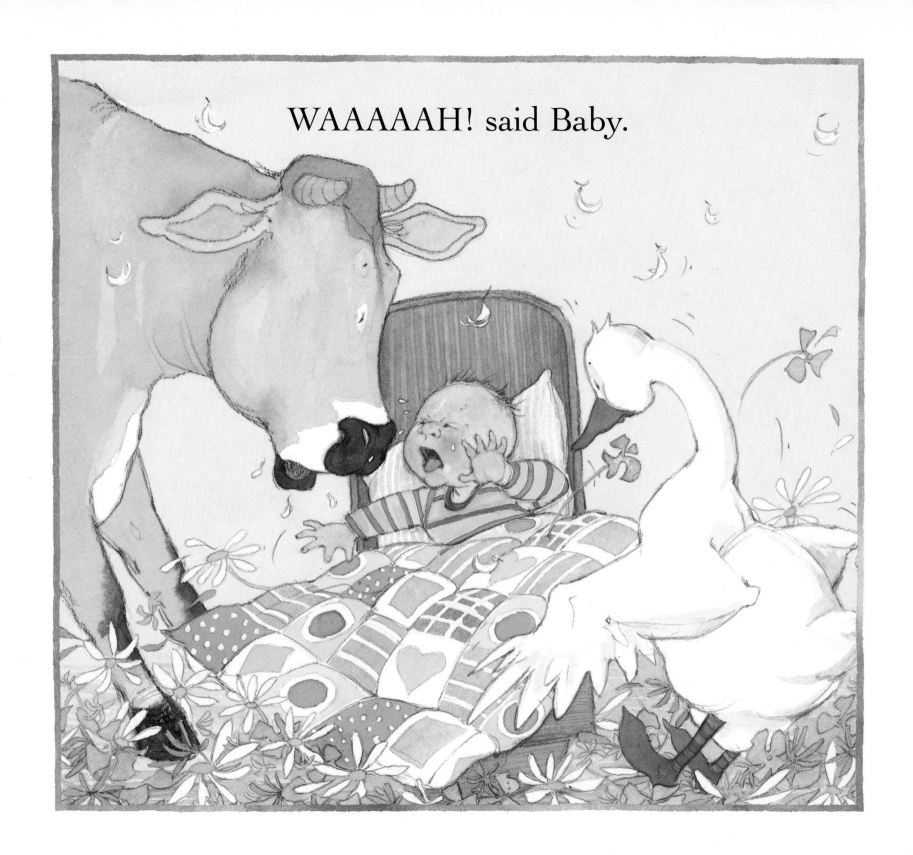

WAAAAAH! said Baby.

"I know what Baby wants!"
said Uncle.
"Baby wants something
to keep him warm."

So Uncle went out to the pasture

and brought Baby a flock of woolly sheep.
Was that what Baby wanted?

Nibbitty, nubbitty,
the sheep nibbled on Baby's hair.

WAAAAAH! said Baby.

"I know what Baby wants!"
said Big Sister.
"Baby wants someone
to sing him to sleep."

So Big Sister went out to the forest

and brought Baby a tree full of birds.
Was that what Baby wanted?

Tawitta, taweeta, the birds
twittered in Baby's ear.

WAAAAAH! said Baby.
WAAAAAH! WAAAAAH!
WAAAAAH!

"Oh, dear," said Grandma and Grandpa
and Aunt and Uncle and Big Sister.
"What *does* Baby want?"

"I think I know what Baby wants,"
said Little Brother.

Little Brother picked Baby up.
He cuddled Baby

and kissed Baby.

He wrapped Baby in his quilt and
sang Baby a soft little lullaby.

Was that what Baby wanted?

Hushabye, shushabye,
Baby's eyes closed.
Baby's crying
stopped.

Just then Papa came home.
"Is everything all right?" he asked.
"Just fine," said Grandma and
Grandpa and Aunt and Uncle
and Big Sister and Little Brother.
"Mama's sleeping, and we're
taking care of Baby."

And they did,
all night long.

PHYLLIS ROOT says, "All parents have experienced the desperation of this situation — their baby won't settle down to go to sleep and they will attempt anything to try to hush the baby. I know I experienced it when my children were babies!" Phyllis Root is the author of many children's books, including *One Duck Stuck* and *Kiss the Cow!*

JILL BARTON grew up spending summers in the country, and she turned to her rural background for inspiration for *What Baby Wants*. She says, "I was inspired by memories of my childhood, especially of my grandparents' farm, and the illustrations for this book just seemed to flow out of the end of my brush." She is the illustrator of many popular children's books, including the award-winning Baby Duck series for Candlewick Press.